LAWN
BOY
RETURNS

ALSO BY GARY PAULSEN

PICTURE BOOKS, ILLUSTRATED BY RUTH WRIGHT PAULSEN

GARY PAULSEN

LAWN
BOY
RETURNS

a yearling book

Text copyright © 2010 by Gary Paulsen
Cover art copyright © 2010 by Pablo Bernasconi

All rights reserved. Published in the United States by Yearling, an imprint of Random House Children's Books, a division of Random House, Inc., New York. Originally published in hardcover in the United States by Wendy Lamb Books, an imprint of Random House Children's Books, a division of Random House, Inc., New York, in 2010.

Yearling and the jumping horse design are registered trademarks of Random House, Inc.

Visit us on the Web! www.randomhouse.com/kids

Educators and librarians, for a variety of teaching tools, visit us at www.randomhouse.com/teachers

The Library of Congress has cataloged the hardcover edition of this work as follows:
Paulsen, Gary.
Lawn Boy returns / Gary Paulsen. — 1st ed.
p. cm.
Summary: Having expanded his summer lawn mowing job into an ever-growing business conglomerate, a twelve-year-old boy gets involved in high finance thanks to his hippie stockbroker, takes on sponsorship of a boxer, and becomes a media sensation.
ISBN 978-0-385-74662-5 (hc) — ISBN 978-0-385-90899-3 (lib. bdg.)
ISBN 978-0-375-89654-5 (ebook)
[1. Business enterprises—Fiction. 2. Humorous stories.] I. Title.
PZ7.P2843 Law 2010
[Fic]—dc22
2009054046

ISBN 978-0-553-49430-3 (pbk.)

Printed in the United States of America

10 9 8 7 6 5 4 3 2 1

First Yearling Edition 2011

Random House Children's Books supports the First Amendment and celebrates the right to read.

*This is for Kathy Dunn Grigo, publicist extraordinaire,
and for Dylan, Ryan and Kaylee Grigo,
for sharing so much of their mother's time with me.*

Foreword

I don't have a clue how all this will end.

There are people who say I'm a wonderboy—one who got jinxed—or that I knew some secret—which I fumbled—or that I had this big, hairy plan.

Nope.

One minute I was twelve years old and wondering where I could get enough money for an inner tube for my old used ten-speed. And the next minute I'm a financial prodigy with my own business and a bunch of people working for me and a stockbroker and a prizefighter of my very own. The minute after that I've got tax problems and

1

employee difficulties and threats of lawsuits and greedy relatives no one's ever heard of before and I'm sick to death of being rich.

Six weeks ago, I inherited my grandfather's old lawn mower and came up with a wild plan of making $7,500 over the twelve weeks of summer if I worked all day, every day, mowing lawns. At the time, it seemed like a staggering amount of money.

Half a summer into my plan, after working really hard, partnering up with another lawn guy, and lucking into Arnold, a customer on my route who was also a genius stock wizard on a hot streak, I was suddenly worth $480,000 from business expansion and stock investments that were, for the most part, happy accidents.

For a little while, it seemed like everything I touched turned to gold. That was the good part.

But then for a little while, it seemed like everything I touched turned to compost. That was the bad part.

I'd better explain.

It all began at nine in the morning on a day in late July, when my grandmother showed up with Joey Pow and his brand-new long-lost cousin Zed.

1

The Origins of
Economic Collapse

I sponsor a great fighter: Joseph Powdermilk, Jr. His nickname is Joey Pow.

My grandmother is the kind of person who always thinks the best of everyone. She's also very big on family.

So when this guy Zed approached Grandma and Joey at the gym and said, "Hey, Joey! It's Zed, your second cousin once removed," Grandma was thrilled.

Joey couldn't hear what the guy was saying because his ears were still ringing from his sparring partner's accidental haymaker. Cousin Zed threw his arm around the still-reeling Joey. "I'm one a yer dad's stepbrother Sam's boys from his second or maybe his third marriage. Could be the seventh one, hard ta keep track a Sam, he's always been what ya call a bad boy, gotta real taste for the ladies."

Grandma beamed at Joey and Joey got all excited because Grandma looked so happy. Grandma hugged Zed and then Zed hugged Joey, and bam, faster than one of Joey's knockouts, Zed had weaseled himself into becoming part of Joey's family.

Over the past few weeks, Grandma and Joey have developed a great and unusual friendship, even though they don't appear to have much in common. She speaks really fast and he talks really slowly; he's enormous and powerful, she's small and gentle. But they're both early birds, which is great because Joey likes to do his workouts at the gym in the morning and Grandma likes to drink coffee and read the newspaper there to the sound of uppercuts to the chin and body punches.

Grandma's learned a lot about boxing recently. I walked in on one of Joey's training sessions the other day and saw her shadowboxing in the corner.

She's been pestering Joey to teach her to feint and jab. Joey likes to have someone look after him, fussing about whether or not he's getting enough sleep and eating enough fiber and all those other grandmotherly things.

That morning, before Zed appeared, my mom and dad had left town for a few days to look at lakefront property up north; Arnold had told us that investing some of my earnings in land would be a good idea. Grandma was staying at our house to keep an eye on me while they were gone, so after Joey's workout she brought Joey and Zed back to my house.

Zed's broken-down pickup truck towed an ancient camper. He parked next to Joey's old station wagon in our driveway.

Grandma is amazing and fun, but there are times when she makes no sense. Still, if you think really hard, you can usually figure out what she means. When she said, "I have always despised the taste and texture of olives," and gestured to this dirty, hairy Zed person as he climbed out of his truck, I couldn't figure out what Zed and olives had in common, but I got a bad feeling.

I think I have a good sense of whether or not a

person can be trusted. For instance, I knew right off the bat that Arnold, my stockbroker, and Pasqual, my lawn-mowing business partner, were good guys. And even though Joey Pow is large and slightly terrifying in appearance, I appreciated his good qualities immediately.

I didn't get the same vibe from Zed.

"Good ta meetcha." Zed stuck his hand out and I forced myself to shake his grubby paw. "Yer granny tol' me how ya sponsor Joey."

"I did?" Grandma looked a little perplexed. "Oh well, it's like I always say: people who are cut from the same cloth can't see the forest for the trees."

"I know a little somethin' about the boxin' biz." Zed threw a few fake punches and zipped his feet back and forth like he was bobbing and weaving to avoid an opponent in the ring.

Grandma beamed at him. Joey wasn't paying any attention; he was petting the neighbor's cat. Next to the cat, Joey looked, as always, ginormous.

I turned back to Zed, who had made himself comfortable in my mother's lawn chair. He leaned back, farted once, burped twice and gave a mighty scratch in an area most parents urge toddlers not to touch in public. Charming. I moved upwind once I caught a whiff of him.

"So, uh, where do you live?" I asked.

"Oh, ya know, here 'n' there. I was passin' through town and heard about my cuz Joey from a buddy."

"Uh-huh. What, exactly, did you hear?"

"I heard Joey's gettin' ready for a big fight. Bruiser Bulk—ain't he the Upper Midwest heavyweight champ? From what I hear, Joey's got a shot at takin' the title."

I looked over at Grandma and Joey. She'd put her hands up in front of her face and Joey was, very gently, tapping them with loose fists as she taunted him. "Is that all you've got? C'mon, let's see some speed and power." Never mind that if Joey so much as flicked her with his forefinger and thumb, he'd propel her into next week.

I looked back at Zed, who had been studying me with the same look that I see in the neighbor's cat's eyes when she watches baby birds learning to fly.

"I heard how ya got stinkin' rich this summer." Zed smiled, and I got a chill down my spine when I saw his teeth. They looked like he'd sharpened them with a file.

I thought: I'm not the only one who needs some-one to keep an eye on them for the next few days.

"So, what do you do for a living?" I asked.

"Oh, ya know, this 'n' that. I'm between jobs now an' it seems to me Joey could use a good corner man, and who's better to have on yer side than fam'ly? Plus I don't go all squeamish at the sighta blood 'n' guts."

Uh-huh.

"Hey, bud." Zed looked around and nodded. "Ya got a nice spread. Figger I can park my rig here? The parkin' lot at Joey's place don't have much room."

"You could, um, probably stay here while you're in town. For a few days. I guess. Because Joey's real busy getting ready for the fight." And I'd rather have you where I can see you, I silently finished. Looking out for Joey's interests was part of my spon-sorship responsibilities.

"That's real sportin' of ya, pal, don't mind if I do." Zed looked way too happy about the chance to park in our driveway.

I broke up Grandma and Joey's boxing lesson. "Zed's going to park here for a few days." Grandma didn't seem to be bothered that we had just brought down the property values of the entire neighborhood

8

by offering to host this rusted-out piece of garbage. Meanwhile, Joey helped Zed plug in the world's longest extension cord from his camper to our garage.

Then Joey took off for his midmorning training session (not to be confused with his early-morning workout and, of course, nothing like his late-morning weight lifting). Grandma went inside to rest her eyes (that's what she calls taking a nap), and Zed—after blowing his nose without using a tissue, sending a snot rocket onto the perfectly mowed lawn—thumped up the step into his "rig" and started to fry up some roadkill he'd scraped off the interstate. At least that's how it smelled.

And that was how the bad part started.

2

The Status Quo in Economic Endeavors—at Best, an Unreliable Concept

I stood on the driveway for a second, wondering: How was I going to handle Zed? Because I had a really strong sense that Zed was a problem. A big problem. Epic. The kind of problem I didn't want a nice guy like Joey to face on his own. I wished I could ask my parents for advice, because they always approach a problem calmly and thoughtfully, but I knew that if I told them about Zed while they were gone, they'd worry about me and Grandma and Joey. And they really deserved a couple of days up north without any worries, because they worked really hard, Dad with all his inventions and Mom teaching math. I wanted them to enjoy the little vacation they'd taken.

Then I glanced at my watch and realized I was running late. I walked into the garage and took the tarp off my lawn mower.

Every evening when I come home from work, I take a rag and wipe all the loose grass and dirt from the riding mower, and then I cover it with a big tarp. I saw a cowboy movie once and was impressed by how the sheriff always brushed his horse and threw a soft blanket over its back at the end of the day. I know I'm no sheriff and my lawn mower isn't a horse, but it just felt like the right thing to do. Crazy, I know, but I'd spent a lot of hours in the seat of my lawn mower and it had been good to me. I owed it to the mower to take good care of it.

I enjoyed five or ten minutes of quiet, just me and my lawn mower. It had started making some weird grinding-buzzing sounds on the drive home last night and I was tinkering with it, trying to re-capture the familiar humming growl I'd come to know like the sound of my own breathing.

"Whatcha doin'?" Kenny Halverson and Allen Grabowksi, my two best friends, came around the

11

corner of the garage and saw me squatting next to the lawn mower. Kenny was dribbling a basketball and Allen had his head buried in a book. I don't know how they do it, but Kenny is always bouncing a ball and Allen is always reading and they never trip or walk into anything.

"Hey!" I stood up. "When did you guys get back?"

"Last night," Kenny said, "and my mother has already told me thirty-seven times to make myself useful, stay out of trouble and stop dribbling the ball in the house."

He lives across the street and around the corner and he'd been at camp for the past month and a half. I knew from his postcards that he and the guys in his cabin had started a hard-core heavy metal headbanging band they called Infected Wound, had gotten in trouble for collecting leeches and applying them to each other's butt cheeks to see if they really did have medicinal properties, and as punishment had been forced to play board games with the camp director's spoiled-rotten seven-year-old grandson. Kenny didn't say whether they'd been punished for the music or the leeches, but since I'd heard him play bass before and Infected Wound was composed of him, three drummers, and a guy who made beat-box noises with his mouth, my money was on the music.

I nodded and turned to Allen. "I got here twenty-seven minutes ago," he said. The thing about Allen is that although he reads a lot, he hardly ever speaks. And when he does, he's precise.

Allen was visiting his dad two blocks away. His parents got divorced two years ago and Allen moved three towns over with his mom. Now he spends half of the summer, every other weekend, Tuesday and Thursday nights and some holidays with his dad.

I was really glad Kenny and Allen were back. But I wondered if I'd have time to hang around with them, since I was working from sunrise until dark. And how would I explain what happened while they were gone? How do you tell your two best buddies that you're a hundred-thousandaire without sounding like you've got a big head about it?

"Wanna shoot hoops?" Kenny bounced the ball between his legs and behind his back.

"Sorry. Can't." I nodded to the mower. "Got work to do."

"Sweet ride," Kenny said. "Where'd you get it?"

"Grandma showed up on my birthday six weeks

ago with Grandpa's old riding mower. I've taken on, oh, a few yard jobs since then."

Kenny knelt on the ground next to me, studying the gas tank and bouncing his basketball off the front wheel. Allen thoughtfully tapped the throttle, where the rabbit and the turtle indicated the two speeds. He propped his book on the steering wheel and nodded. "Good fit."

"And so, uh, I've got this, um, little business now." I'd ease them into the big picture gradually.

"Need any help?" Kenny asked. "Allen and I haven't got anything better to do, and it'll be fun to make a few bucks. We don't have riding mowers, but our dads have lawn mowers just sitting there in our garages, and I bet the three of us working together could make some serious coin."

Like four hundred and eighty thousand dollars? I asked him silently. I smiled. "Let's do it. Go get your mowers and I'll meet you at the corner of Hubbard and Noble. I've got to tighten a few bolts here."

As soon as they left, I made some calls. I let Pasqual and Louis, one of our most trustworthy employees, who was taking on more responsibility all the time, know that I'd be handling the Gorens' yard myself that morning. It was the closest account to my house, and it was an enormous corner lot that I figured would give Kenny and Allen a better sense of the work involved. Plus, there'd be no risk we'd run into any of the guys who worked for me. Introducing my friends to my employees was going to be a seriously weird moment that I'd just as soon avoid for a while longer.

And then I called Arnold to check in. He asked me to swing by the house later that afternoon; he had a few ideas he wanted to run past me.

I figured I'd find the right way to introduce my two best friends to my stockbroker. Arnold was very laid-back and had a way of making the incredible sound almost sane, so I felt good about how that scene would most likely play out.

We had a blast that morning in the Gorens' yard.

Sure, Allen almost cut his left foot off because he "got to a really good part" in the book he was reading and rammed the mower into some paving bricks along the front path, and Kenny thought it would be fun for us to race each other up and down the hill alongside the driveway pushing the mowers, blindfolded, and he knocked the mailbox down trying to beat me. (I texted Pasqual when Kenny wasn't looking. Pasqual was in charge of the finer points of lawn care and promised to come over and repair the damage later that night.) The yard, which would have taken me forty-eight minutes by myself, took us three hours and twenty-six minutes to finish and looked pretty ratty along the fence (another secret text to Pasqual about *that*).

But I remembered (a) how much fun it can be to hang with my buddies and (b) what a great feeling a person gets from good, old-fashioned hard work. Change is good, but sometimes leaving things the way they've always been is better.

3

The Methodology of
Team Development

After we were done working on the Gorens' yard,
we dropped off the push mowers and drove to the
Burger Barn for lunch, Allen and Kenny clinging to
the sides of my mower because you're not allowed to
walk up to the drive-through window. No one ever
said anything about lawn mowers being prohibited,
though. We screamed our orders into the speaker
over the whine of the idling engine and, when we
putt-putted around the corner to pick up our food,
we cracked up at the look on the window girl's face.
She laughed too.

We raced each other to the park halfway between the Burger Barn and Arnold's house. Allen and Kenny made better time walking—Kenny backwards and dribbling his basketball and Allen forwards but reading—than I did on the lawn mower. After we snarfed our burgers and fries and onion rings, I told them, "Okay, let's go meet a friend of mine." And then we pointed the lawn mower in the direction of Arnold's house.

When I walked in with Allen and Kenny, Arnold was sitting on his screened-in porch at his round picnic table drinking his hippie tea with four strangers, two men and two women. "Groovy, you're here. And you brought friends. Far out." Arnold pulled extra chairs out from the kitchen and practically fell over himself shaking Allen's and Kenny's hands, introducing himself and pouring three more glasses of tea.

When Arnold told them he was my stockbroker, Kenny and Allen looked at him, at me, at each of the four people sitting at the table and at each other and raised their eyebrows. Then they sat down.

Arnold began to speak.

"Given the dramatic—and, may I add, unprecedented—expansion of your financial assets and professional interests this summer, which is, of course, trippy and wild, I think we need to discuss adding to the team. I've done some research and found four people I think you should meet."

I remembered the last time Arnold thought I should meet someone: Pasqual. And then I pictured the other fourteen people Pasqual had brought on board as we had expanded our services from mowing lawns to also doing cleanup at night—because some of our employees worked other jobs in the daytime but needed the extra income—as well as shrub trimming, pool cleaning, sidewalk edging and garage cleaning. I braced myself as Arnold introduced his other guests.

Allen and Kenny looked slightly terrified to find themselves in a business meeting. Kenny patted his basketball nervously and Allen absentmindedly thumbed through his book. Their eyes were fixed on Arnold.

"Savannah's the best accountant in town," Arnold said.

Good, I thought, because I shouldn't settle for second best.

"Lindy is an up-and-coming attorney."

Well, that's just perfect, inasmuch as I am up-and-coming too.

"Frank is the most efficient business manager I've ever met."

I nodded. Doesn't every soon-to-be-seventh-grader need a good business manager?

"And Gib is an administrative assistant without peer," Arnold finished.

Which is swell, since I'm at the point in my career where I shouldn't hire employees with peer.

Kenny was sitting with the basketball forgotten in his lap, and, miracle of miracles, Allen had set his book aside. They were both slack-jawed. I remembered feeling like that all the way back in early June.

"I guess," Kenny finally said slowly, "the butler, chauffeur and personal chef couldn't make this meeting?"

"No," Arnold started, before he saw Kenny's grin. "Oh, right, ha! I guess this comes as a surprise if you haven't been here since the start."

"Surprise?" Allen said carefully.

I held my breath and waited to see how they rolled with the idea that the guy they went trick-or-treating with was a businessman who had, as Kenny would put it, serious coin.

Allen leaned forward. "So, Arnold, what's the next step?"

"And," Kenny said, "how can we help?"

Grandma once said, "If you have good friends, you can consider yourself truly wealthy." Of course, she was replying to my question about why we turned the clocks back in the fall.

At that moment, I knew exactly what she'd been talking about.

4

The Prudence of Adding Personnel to Manage Material and Financial Well-being

"I'm glad you asked." Arnold beamed at Allen. "Since everyone will be, initially, part-time, they'll set up shop in my house. I'm not a proponent of wasting money on rent. So until we can find a solid building to buy to accommodate the administrative portions of the operations as well as to create equity through property ownership, I think we should keep reinvesting the profits in stocks and focus on expanding the employee base."

Well, sure, when he put it like that, I could see that I was never going to become a preteen real estate mogul if I wasted earnings by renting rather than buying.

Like I had a clue.

But Allen nodded like he wrestled with the rent-versus-buy dilemma every day. And Kenny was sliding his chair closer to Savannah.

Arnold turned to them and, as if he'd somehow *known* that I'd be bringing my buddies to this meeting and had a plan in mind, said, "I'm glad to have you two on board at this critical point of the development and extension of the brand. Allen, I'd like you in-house to help me keep things running here at the command post, and Kenny, if you could work in the field with Pasqual and Louis to assist the yard crews, that'd be far out.

"Here's a laptop." Arnold handed me a shiny silver rectangle. "I loaded it with our bookkeeping, scheduling, word processing and address book programs. The systems are linked between the six of us and the entire network is password-protected.

"Gib will look after things so you can concentrate on the lawn-mowing operation and, of course, school in the fall."

He's right. I can't worry about the phases of my operations when I've got a trig test to study for.

Trig looms in my life like a mathematical predatory beast.

"Savannah and I will set up quarterly tax payments and establish a trust to protect your savings and start your college account. And, of course, a retirement plan."

I've been wondering, at age twelve, about my retirement.

"Lindy's drawing up articles of incorporation, which will protect your personal assets from any real or perceived vulnerabilities or liabilities of a professional nature."

Can a seventh grader sign legal documents? My parents won't even let me buy the super-hyper-energy drink at the convenience store.

"And," Arnold said, "since you're a minor, we'll set up your parents with powers of attorney. I've already talked to them about some financial issues and they're up to speed, but this will legalize the situation."

I hoped Mom would be in charge of whatever the power of attorney thing was. Dad is great, but he's an inventor and he'd probably tune out while he sketched gigantic catapults and estimated the tensile strength required for a bungee cord to send a one-man glider into orbit. Dad gets carried away with his inventions; Mom's a math teacher so she zeroes right in on things.

"Frank will be the go-to guy for everyone. He'll liaise with all divisions and serve as the point man between key players. He'll input and update all the facts and figures and forward you and the team weekly status reports."

Liaise? What kind of word was that?

I studied Arnold while he passed around matching leather notebooks. A funny little round man in hippie clothes with a mind like a steel trap.

It didn't look like I needed to stay for the next part of the meeting. "Thanks, everyone." I stood. "Let's go," I said to Kenny and Allen.

But Allen was making notes in the notebook I'd left on the table. He looked right at home.

Kenny leaned toward Savannah. "How do you start a college fund?" It had to be the first time Kenny had even *thought* about college.

As I was halfway out the door, Arnold handed me a new BlackBerry. "Check this regularly, okay? We'll meet up with everyone tonight at Joey Pow's big fight. Sitting together in the sponsor's box will be a bonding experience for the team."

Bonding. Team. Sure.

Kenny's eyes popped. "You sponsor a prizefighter?"

Allen flipped to the section in the notebook that covered Joey. His lips moved when he read, though, so I knew he was a little rattled by all this news.

I drove home and into the garage, shut the door and sat on my lawn mower in the dim light to think. Some people take yoga classes or meditate, but for me, sitting on the lawn mower helps make sense of things. There's something about looking at the picture of the turtle and the rabbit on the throttle that puts everything in perspective.

Right now life was in rabbit mode.

If Mr. Bunny had been taking human growth hormones and was overly caffeinated.

5

The Code of Conduct for Dispute Resolution

I was still sitting in the garage, at one with my lawn mower, feeling a little overwhelmed . . . okay, a lot overwhelmed . . . okay, completely terrified and panicked, when I heard a racket in the driveway.

I peeked out one of the garage door windows and saw Zed outside his camper, playing air guitar to the radio blasting from his pickup cab, a bag of lard-soaked, deep-fat-fried pork rinds and a six-pack of beer on the ground at his side. He chugged two cans at once, lifted his head like a wolf baying at the moon and let loose with a burp so loud it must have deafened house pets three houses over.

Truly a class act.

When were my parents getting home? And what would Zed look like stuffed in the passenger side of his pickup upside down and bent double? That was what Joey Pow had done to some bad guys who tried to mess with us once.

Joey. I'd go to the gym to see Joey. He has a wonderfully clear and simple outlook on life and is extremely comforting to be around. Plus, I wanted to spend some time with my fighter before his big match.

"Hey, bro," Zed yelled over the hum of the electric garage door opener and the growl of the lawn mower's engine as I drove out, "wouldja lend me a coupla bucks?"

I pretended I couldn't hear, gesturing to my ears and shrugging as I rumbled past him and took a hard right onto the street.

"Hello, sponsor. You seem sad," Joey said when I got to the gym. He leaped out of the ring. His agility is surprising, because he's so big he makes gardening sheds seem tiny.

"Oh, I'm okay, I guess, I just— Wait! Is that Rock over there?"

28

Rock was a guy who'd given us some trouble a few weeks ago when he wanted to buy me out of my lawn-mowing business without, of course, any money changing hands. Joey made that problem go away by bowling, with Rock and some of his guys as the ball and the pins.

"He works for me now."

"Doing what?"

"Whatever I tell him. Now he is cleaning out slop buckets, and later he will scrub the urinals. The little cakes get dirty in the urinals. It is good to have them clean. The little blue cakes. In the urinals."

"But why does he work for you?"

"He needed"—Joey stopped to think—"supervision."

Well, will wonders never cease.

"Arnold told me how you make deals and have employees. Now so do I."

I watched Joey smile at Rock, who flinched. Rock had a slight limp and two big Joey-sized handprint bruises on his upper arms, as if he'd been picked up and moved.

"Uh, hey, Joey? What do you think about Zed?"

"I think Zed is shifty."

"You do?"

"Yes. He has pinchy eyes. That is not a good thing."

"He doesn't give off the best energy," I agreed.

"Besides"—Joey took a deep breath—"I don't have an uncle Sam."

"Then why are you going along with him pretending to be your cousin?"

"Like Rock, he needs to be watched. And I'm good at handling trouble."

"I know." I must have looked worried, though, because Joey patted me on the head. If the pats had been just a tad firmer, he could have pat-pat-patted me right into the ground.

"Don't think about Zed. Or Rock," he said. "Today we think about Bruiser Bulk and the fight."

"How are you feeling about the match tonight?"

"I have"—he paused to study the floor as if the word he needed could be found somewhere near his left shoe—"concerns."

"About what?"

He looked at me sadly. Then he looked at Rock. Then he shook his head. "You leave the fight to me. I'll make you proud."

"I'm always real proud of you, Joey."

His smile could have lit up a room.

"Oh, good, there you are." I heard Grandma's happy voice from the doorway. We turned and, if I hadn't been standing so close to Joey, I'd have fallen to the ground.

Grandma's hair was red. Not red like Little Orphan Annie or Lucille Ball. Red like Bozo the Clown. Red like a fire truck. Red like all the red in the entire history of the whole universe had been concentrated on her head. Her hair glowed. And shimmered. When she moved, I could see . . . sparkles. The brightness made me wince.

"Do you love it?" She twirled proudly. Joey and I squinted and took a step back. Toward a dark corner. Hoping Grandma and her head would follow us out of the light. "I colored it myself today. I was at the drugstore buying ice—did you know that I only like store-bought ice? Homemade ice tastes funny and makes my tea smell strange."

"Grandma. Your hair?"

"Oh, right, well, anyway, I was buying ice and I wandered down the hair dye aisle and these boxes were on sale for seventy-nine cents so I bought four. Germaine would have charged me way more than that at the salon. And you just *know* she'd never have gotten this shade. Do you realize that I exactly match Joey Pow's boxing trunks?"

"Did you use all four boxes?"

"Yes. It took all four boxes to get this color. I spent all day in the bathroom doing my hair."

I bet.

I mentally kicked myself for having forgotten about Grandma all day. The last time I'd seen her was earlier that morning after she arrived at my house with Zed. She'd gone to take a nap, and—well, even for Grandma, who loves resting her eyes like most people love converting oxygen to carbon dioxide, that wasn't an all-day proposition.

"What's that?" I suspiciously eyed the spray bottle she pulled out of her purse.

"Diluted leftover dye. C'mere, sweetie, and let me spritz you so that you have Joey Pow red hair too."

"No, thanks, I'm good with brown."

"Suit yourself." Grandma shoved the spray bottle back into her purse and looked at her watch. I don't know why, because it's broken. But she says she feels lost without it, and she won't get it fixed because her wrist would feel naked while the watch was at the repair place. "We'd better get to the auditorium if we don't want to miss the fight. And did I ever tell you that those little sticky notes were really an accident when someone was trying to come up with adhesive?" She sailed off, a beacon of red, toward the back door and her car. I've driven with Grandma before, so I was just as happy to hitch a ride with Joey. I turned to him; he was looking after Grandma, smiling.

"Grandma is wonderful." He tore off his gloves with his teeth and gathered his gear in a duffel bag.

"Wonderful. Colorful. Whatever. C'mon, Joe, we've got to get going or we'll be late for your fight."

He grabbed Rock on the way out. Literally. Reached over, plucked Rock off the bench where he'd been cowering and reeking of urinal cakes and dragged him behind us like a toddler dragging a security blanket.

6

Brains Good,
Brawn Sometimes Better

Joey and Rock and I enjoyed a silent ride to the auditorium downtown. Joey dropped me off at the VIP door and I flashed my sponsor's badge at the guard. Joey and Rock drove around the back entrance to the locker room.

I spotted Grandma near the ring right away. I wished I'd worn sunglasses. She was chatting with Arnold, Kenny and Allen. They're not shy, but they were all looking at the ground while they talked with her. The glare from her head was too much for them.

Savannah, Gib, Frank and Lindy huddled together, each of them frantically thumb-typing on their BlackBerrys. Were they tending to my empire even during a social event? That was good, because I was taking the evening off to enjoy the fight. I turned around and saw Pasqual, Louis and Benny—who'd started working for us a week before and was fast becoming indispensable—and their wives. Behind them were about twelve guys from the yard crew. We all high-fived each other.

We took our seats in the sponsor's box, which was the two front rows behind Joey's corner of the ring. Kenny and Allen almost lost their minds when Arnold told them that the concession food was free to my guests. They ordered one of everything. I was too nervous to eat; I kept remembering how sad Joey had been when he'd talked about the fight earlier that day. I'm new to the prizefighting game, but there was something about the look in his eye that worried me.

After what felt like forever, the houselights went down and an announcer's voice boomed through the auditorium, introducing the two fighters, who entered the arena from the locker rooms on opposite sides. In one spotlight, I saw Joey in his red robe and trunks. He was dragging Rock after him. Zed swaggered behind, bringing up the rear.

Zed.

I felt a nasty chill run up my spine. Why did I get such a bad feeling from this guy? Besides the fact that he was a dirty, lying mooch, of course.

I ran over to the corner and shouted in Joey's ear over the roar of the crowd, "What's Zed doing here?"

"While I fight, Zed and Rock can supervise each other."

The audience booed and cheered as Bruiser Bulk climbed into the ring. He looked like he'd been carved from stone. Tattooed stone. He moved slowly around his corner, muscles rippling on his body where I hadn't known muscles existed. He made his first and middle fingers into a V and pointed first at his own eyes and then at Joey, as if to say, "I see you. I see you and I'm going to eat you for breakfast." Joey didn't notice; he was waving at Grandma.

The introductions of the fighters ("In this corner, wearing black trunks, the Upper Midwest heavyweight champ, Bah-ruuuuuuiser Bullllllllllllllllllk! And, in the opposite corner, his opponent, wearing

red trunks, Jo-o-o-o-o-o-o-o-o-o-ey Po-o-o-ow!")
took longer than the actual fight.

One right roundhouse.

One left uppercut.

One right punch in the face that made an ugly
splat.

Four and a half seconds.

Three lightning-fast blows followed by a *thunk* as
Bruiser Bulk hit the canvas.

Joey Pow worked so fast that I hadn't even gotten back to my seat; I was still standing near his corner of the ring, between Rock, who looked worried,
and Zed, who looked furious.

The ref knelt next to Bruiser, counting to nine
and checking to make sure he was breathing. When
the ref got to nine, he leaped up, grabbed Joey's arm
and raised it above their heads.

"The. Newwwwwwwwww. Upperrrrrrrrrrrrrrrr. Mid-
wessssssssssst. Heavyweight. Chammmmmmmmmpion.
JO-O-O-O-O-O-O-O-O-O-O-O-EY   PO-O-O-O-
O-O-O-O-O-O-O-O-O-OW!"

I'd have gone with "JOEEEEEEEEEEEEEEEEEY
PO-O-O-O-O-O-OW," but it still sounded good.

Allen and Kenny were jumping up and down
screaming, making it snow popcorn. Grandma was

standing on her chair, howling like a wolf, and Arnold was smiling and shaking hands with everyone in his vicinity. Savannah, Gib, Frank and Lindy were texting like someone's life depended on it.

Zed went flying out of the auditorium, Rock hot on his heels. Before I could even think about following them to see what was going on, Joey rumbled over to hug me and squeezed so hard I felt some of my ribs move.

"Excuse me. Joey Pow?" A woman interrupted our celebration. She was holding a microphone. A guy carrying a television camera on his shoulder stood behind her. "I'm Sandra Santana, sports reporter from Action News 7. We'd like to interview you."

"Hello. I am Joey Pow. I am beating all my opponents in four and a half seconds. It is because I wear the red trunks my sponsor says are good luck. This is my sponsor."

"You?" Sandra Santana raised her eyebrows and turned the mike to me. A blinding light atop the camera flashed on. Between Grandma's hair and the TV lights, I'd be seeing flashing swirly dots in front of my eyes for years.

7

The Detrimental Influence of Fame and the Loss of Privacy as a Result of Prosperity

"I'll have to give serious thought to bringing a PR person on board," Arnold said to me the next morning. "Someone to handle the media and coach you about what to say in public."

That was probably a sound idea, since I couldn't imagine giving another interview, the first one having been so unexpected and terrifying. My tongue was still stuck to the roof of my mouth. Which tasted like—well, never mind. It was bad.

I'd appeared as a feature on the ten o'clock news the night before, the little human-interest story they do between the weather and sports. Sandra Santana had asked me all kinds of questions about why I had become a prizefighter's sponsor and how I'd made the money in the first place and who was the genius stockbroker who'd made me rich.

The bright lights and her fast questions made me nervous and confused and I couldn't remember what I'd said two seconds earlier. She forgot all about her interview with Joey, who didn't seem to mind; he stood next to me, his arm around my shoulders, beaming. It was only a two-minute piece, but it felt like I stood there for an agonizingly long time, dripping sweat under lights hotter than a blowtorch.

Grandma and I woke up the next morning to a bunch of neighbors on the front lawn taking pictures of our house. I was especially proud that they got such good shots of Zed's camper and his laundry, mostly made up of skidmarked underwear, which he had drying on the line he'd strung between his radio antenna and the garage light. Luckily, Zed slept through the excitement, so they didn't get a picture of him in his tightie whities and bedhead.

And there were also a bunch of girls about my age who wanted my autograph. I like girls, but I can't talk to them. Not a word. Turns out you don't have to talk when you sign autographs, and they smile and are nice to you anyway. Sweet.

By 9:47 that morning, Arnold had received numerous calls about me.

"The local university has invited you to lecture to their econ department, the newspaper wants to do a series on you and me and our working arrangement, several Internet teen sites have expressed interest in having you blog for them, and the big cable sports channel wants to fly you and Joey to New York to be on their round-table program Sunday morning."

"I don't know about any of that. . . . I mean, what to do . . ."

"Wait, there's more." He studied a fistful of messages.

Real good. I was so hoping there would be more. More was what I was lacking in my life. I needed more *more* around here. I started to get dizzy.

"We've also gotten an offer from a national lawn fertilizer company for you to endorse their new organic mix. Who knew all poop wasn't organic— they have plastic cows? And a swimming pool company wants to pay you to use your picture on their trucks because of the high-quality pool cleaning you're known for. A licensing company wants to be the official supplier of Lawn Boy T-shirts, lunch boxes, thermoses, caps, water bottles, sunglasses, sunscreen, lawn bags, gardening tools and, for some reason, giant foam fingers."

"Um . . ."

"Oh yeah, and can you run outside when we're done talking here and sign autographs for those girls sitting on the curb waiting for you with their autograph books? They've been here since I woke up. I sent Kenny and Allen out to deal with them when they arrived this morning, but I think the girls are waiting for you."

I peeked out Arnold's window. This latest batch of girls were cute. Maybe even cuter than the girls in my front yard. Kenny was spinning his basketball on his forefinger as he talked to three or four of them. Allen and some curly-headed girl were sitting on the curb sharing a book. Good; Kenny and Allen would make it way easier to face all those girls.

I turned back to Arnold, who was still talking.

"We've also gotten a call from an entrepreneur

in Texas who wants to talk to you about the possibility of opening nationwide franchises."

"What does that mean?"

"Like what you set up here with Pasqual. You lend your name to the company and they start up subdivisions of lawn care, shrub trimming, pool cleaning, sidewalk edging and garage cleaning services, from which you receive royalties and other fees."

"Arnold. I don't feel so well."

"But this is groovy. Capitalism plus publicity equals monster commerce."

"And that's a good thing?"

"That's a far-out, trippy thing." He waved his whole body back and forth in place, like a round little willow tree bending in a gentle breeze. "It makes the world, like, move."

The world wasn't the only thing moving. My dizziness was getting worse, and not only was Arnold waving, but there were two—no, wait, three of him.

I knew that the only thing that would settle me down was to do a few lawns. As soon as Arnold turned to answer a question from Gib, I slipped out the kitchen door to the garage, crawled through the side window and shinnied down the wall next to the overgrown lilac bush. I squatted in the branches and texted Pasqual: NEED TO WORK; GIVE ME AN ADDRESS.

As soon as I got his reply, 4024 BROADWAY, I commando-crawled through the bushes to the corner of the garage and, waiting until the coast was clear—the autograph girls were talking to Allen and Kenny, and I couldn't be spotted by anyone in the house—I sprinted through Arnold's backyard and cut through the Sautters' side yard and came out on the street a block away.

I walk-trotted back to my own street, where, hiding behind Mrs. Steck's sheets hanging on her clothesline next door, I made sure Zed was nowhere in sight. Then I jogged to the garage and my lawn mower. While sitting on the mower, I did some deep-breathing exercises we'd learned in gym class, until the panicky dread in my gut had subsided a little.

Then I shoved the throttle to turtle and headed off to work. I'd feel better after I'd done a yard or two.

8

The Model of
Capricious Development

The interview fallout picked up steam, and the next day Arnold insisted that I spend the day with him rather than working on lawns. He sent Kenny to take my place working with Pasqual and the guys. Gib and Frank went to full-time positions. Arnold made an offer on the building he thought I should buy to house our operations. And he hired a PR person named Kathy who answered and made and returned a lot of phone calls and then typed up itineraries for interviews and appearances.

Gib, Frank and Kathy set up shop in what had once been Arnold's living room, using the dining room table and dragging the kitchen table in too. Savannah and Lindy kept stopping by with papers to go over with Arnold and for me to give to my parents for signatures. Everyone had BlackBerrys pressed to their heads and there was a sea of cables underfoot for all the computers and printers and copiers they'd brought in.

It was . . . well, groovy. If, of course, your definition of groovy is sensory overload.

Arnold worked on the screened-in porch, sitting peacefully at his round picnic table drinking his sweet hippie tea and making money while he tap-tap-tapped on his keyboard. Allen was never far away, watching him, then tapping on *his* laptop. I looked over Allen's shoulder and saw that he was creating pie charts and bar graphs and all sorts of other things that we used in math class last term and that didn't make any sense to me but seemed to make Allen really happy.

Kathy had started a Web site for me and asked me to write "copy" for it. Apparently, Web pages are nothing without "content."

"Just write your story in your own words," she said. "People want to get to know who you are."

What she posted was nothing I had written. She

had a better sense of what made me me than I did. She made me sound smarter and not nearly as confused as I really was. Lately, I was feeling just this side of a drooling idiot.

Kathy took a bunch of pictures of me and sent Frank off to get shots of the work crews and Joey. She also took a couple of pictures of the girls waiting on the curb for me to sign autographs. "Content combined with visuals," she explained, "makes for a captivating site."

At one point she came running to find me and asked, "How do you feel about the possibility of reality TV? Camera crews will follow you around and you'll be a prime-time series."

"I'll puke."

"Oh." She didn't ask again.

A box arrived in the office in the afternoon: Team Lawn Boy T-shirts and uniform pants, and truck magnets for the crew to slap on their pickups. That was the best part of my day, driving around with Gib (not officially a chauffeur, but the go-to guy when I had to go to someplace) and handing the stuff out to all the guys.

I breathed deep every time we stopped at a job site, smelling the fresh-cut grass, and thought back to how simple and pure my life had been when I mowed lawns as a summer job.

Was it just a month or so ago?

I was glad my parents were out of cell range. They don't watch television, and I knew they wouldn't bother with newspapers while they were up north. So they wouldn't know that in the past forty-eight hours I had become what Kathy called a media sensation.

"You're bigger," she told me, "than sliced bread."

"What does that mean?"

"It's a good thing. Don't worry."

9

Social and Ethical
Responsibilities
of Management

Arnold tried to talk to me the next morning about
"establishing and implementing our official poli-
cies on hiring and firing, salary and wage structure,
health and life insurance coverage, retirement, sick
days, vacation, and incentive-based performance
bonuses for employees."

It was very exciting.

I think.

I was having a hard time focusing because I'd
just spent the better part of a mind-numbing hour in
the office/dining room with some of my employees

and, as I explained to Arnold a little peevishly, I didn't feel like giving them anything.

"Why do you feel that way?" he asked.

"As best I understand things: Lindy has a crush on Frank, who is sweet on Savannah, who is mad at Gib for not handing in receipts promptly, and Gib resents Frank for overstepping his role as business manager. Oh, and Frank thinks Gib is a slacker, while Lindy is peeved at Savannah for her very existence, because, as Gib explained to me, if Savannah wasn't around, Frank would appreciate all that Lindy has to offer. And Kenny doesn't want to go out and work on lawns anymore because he'd rather sit around mooning after Savannah."

"That is not groovy at all."

"Really."

"Numbers are so clean and elegant; people are so messy and complicated." Arnold sighed. "I know! We'll get an office manager once we move into the new office space. Someone who can keep things totally cool." He gestured to Allen, who wrote down OFFICE MANAGER in the small notebook he carried. Allen was always writing down things Arnold said.

"You're saying we actually need someone to manage the people who are working for us to manage the business?"

"Crazy, isn't it? But just think—you're stimulating the economy by giving all these people jobs."

"But who's going to manage the people we hire to manage the people who manage the business?"

"Oh. Well . . . wait. You're kidding now, right? Because we don't really need to have people manage the people who manage the people who manage the business. That would be just silly."

"Good."

He studied me for a moment. "How do you think Kathy is doing?"

There was a strange sound in his voice. I looked at him quickly, then away. Oops. He had that look. The same one that Lindy got when Frank walked into the room and the same one that Frank and Kenny got when they saw Savannah.

I probably shouldn't tell Arnold that I heard Kathy on the phone with her boyfriend, Kurt. Must keep up morale.

"She's busy. She wants us to do a phoner.

Whatever that means. With a commercially geo-marketed syndicated radio show. Whatever *that* means. Today. But you know, I'm feeling like I need some fresh air so I don't get any more confused and, you know, run screaming into the lake. I rode my lawn mower over and I think I'll go out and do a few lawns, just to clear my head."

"Good." Arnold had started sorting through a thick pile of envelopes. "You do that. Then come back in the afternoon so we can touch base again."

Right, I thought. So we can touch base.

Before I headed off to do some yards, I turned to Allen. "You should take the rest of the day off and drag Kenny out of the living room and away from Savannah."

Allen jumped up. He looked relieved. Kenny was in another room, sitting by the window like a lonely house pet, waiting for Savannah to come back to the office from an appointment.

"I think you both need a change of scenery," I went on. "Go to the state fair. Eat deep-fried things on sticks. See the freak show. Maybe ask a couple of the autograph girls from the front curb to go.

There's nothing like a corn dog and a bearded lady to make you forget about work."

I wished I could go with them, but even more than curly fries and a look at the beauty queen carved life-sized in butter, I needed to work a few lawns today.

10

The Juxtaposition of Financial Status and Jurisprudence

I signed a few autographs on the way out of Arnold's driveway, then mowed a few lawns, ate lunch with Louis and his crew, and headed back to the office.

I walked through Arnold's front door and a lady in a suit and too much red lipstick jumped up from the couch. She shrieked, "There he is, poor child!" and pulled me into a hug that nearly jammed the brass buttons on her jacket through my head.

I peeked over at Arnold for an explanation as she said, "Hi, sweetie, I'm a civil rights attorney and

I heard about your terrible plight on the news. Don't you worry about a thing from now on, because I've already filed a lawsuit on your behalf. I'm suing your parents for violation of child labor laws and having them served with papers immediately upon their return from this inexplicable vacation they've taken without you. I'm thinking of reporting them for desertion of a minor child as well," she finished in a huff.

Arnold seemed to have shrunk with each word.

Then she did that gross thing where she licked her thumb and was about to rub some dirt off my cheek, but I leaped away from her.

And crashed into a fat guy with a ponytail who was holding a bulging briefcase.

"Who are you?"

"I'm the attorney who wants to represent you in your emancipation suit against your parents. Don't listen to that ambulance chaser"—he gestured toward the lipstick lady—"you're, what, twelve? Too old to be treated like a child, but plenty old enough to sue for your right to control your own money. I think the youngest plaintiff in a successful litigation of an emancipation suit was fifteen, maybe sixteen, but we have a good case."

Arnold had started to look like he might blow away.

"You both want me to sue my *parents?*"

"Yes." They spoke in unison and then glared at each other.

"The wheels are already in motion," Lipstick Lady said. "In fact, the matter is out of your hands; it's up to the courts to determine what's in your best interests now."

"Don't listen to her," Ponytail Guy said. "She finished at the bottom of her online law school class and doesn't know what she's talking about. We'll file an injunction against her suit when we file your suit before she can file an injunction against our suit to stop our suit and injunction to stop her suit. Now, if you'll just sign here where I've indicated with an X."

"Please." Miraculously, Arnold had regained his previous size and composure. "Leave the papers with our executive assistant and we'll appraise the points you've raised at our soonest convenience. Thank you."

He all but shoved them out the front door. He locked it and turned to me.

"Let's sit on the porch and have some tea. We have a lot to talk about."

I got the distinct feeling that when he said "a lot," what he meant was "something brand-new."

Uh-oh.

11

The Recognition of a Diminishing Rate of Return

When we were seated at Arnold's picnic table, I said, "Give it to me straight."

"The quarterly tax payments that Savannah filed triggered an audit by the Internal Revenue Service."

Oh, is that all?

"Seems the tax people are alarmed by your sudden, and dramatic, appearance on their radar. Usually, that kind of money stems from illegal activities, especially when the paper trail is so complicated and diverse.

"Your assets are in a slight, some might say a

58

teeny-tiny, bit of danger of being frozen until every-thing is settled."

I wasn't too panicked, since I'd actually never seen the money after the first few weeks, when I had crammed wads of cash into my pockets. Now all the money existed solely as digits on a computer screen.

"Can the crews still work? I'd hate for them to lose money."

"Sure. Pasqual will collect the money from the clients as always, pay the workers and then deposit your portion into the bank account. Even if it does become frozen, you can still make deposits, you just can't make withdrawals. If necessary, I'll cover salaries for Frank and Lindy and Gib and Savannah until we get this muddle straightened out. I'll make sure Joey Pow is okay too."

"What a mess."

"Don't worry, we've filed an emergency appeal."

"How long will that take?"

"Well, since we're claiming this is an emergency and that many livelihoods are at stake, I'd say three to six months."

"How long does it take if they don't think it's urgent?"

"Don't ask. But in that case . . . maybe your grandchildren could get some money."

"Ah."

"Yes."

This, I thought, has been a very interesting day.

12

The Entire Organization Imperiled by a Threat, Perceived or Real, to One Part

Arnold and I were sitting quietly. I was trying not to barf on his picnic table.

All I had wanted was a new inner tube for my ten-speed, which I never got to ride anymore anyway, and now all this had happened.

In my mind's eye, I could picture Allen and Kenny at the state fair, probably riding the Ferris wheel and eating ginormous wads of cotton candy and dragging around ratty stuffed animals they'd won at the milk can throw. Would I ever have fun again?

Money problems for someone my age are supposed to be about not having any, not about having so much that the feds come after you.

And here I'd thought telling Kenny and Allen I was rich had been tricky. Wait until Mom and Dad got home and I had to break it to them that my finances were being audited. Or frozen. Or audited and then frozen. Whatever. It was not the kind of news you broke to your parents over the phone; this called for face time when they got back from up north.

I thought about talking to Grandma in the meantime, but she'd probably just tell me not to go swimming until an hour after I ate.

And I would have liked to talk to Joey, but he might handle the trouble by pinching heads at the tax office. Nope, I was on my own with this one.

Oh, well, I thought, it's only money. It's not like anything really bad has happened.

That was when Rock showed up on the back porch.

"We have trouble," he announced.

I don't know about anyone else, but thirty seconds without bad news and I'm bored.

"What kind of trouble, and what do you mean 'we'?" Arnold and I asked at the same time.

"Joey Pow wasn't supposed to win. Some rough people wanted Bruiser to win. They told Joey Pow to throw the fight or else   "

"Or else what?"

Rock flinched. "I don't know if he forgot to lose or if he just doesn't have it in him to be dishonest or if he didn't want to let you down, but now these guys are mad. They lost a lot of money on the fight and . . ." Rock trailed off.

"Why are *you* telling us?" I asked.

"You've got no reason to trust me after our prior dealings, I understand, but Joey, well, he's a good person and these are guys I used to know and it's your grandmother they threatened."

"*Grandma?*" I jumped up. "What are they going to do to my grandmother?"

"Well, nothing, since Joey hasn't let her out of his sight."

I breathed a sigh of relief. Okay, Grandma was safe, but if they had come after Joey once, they'd come after him again. Joey was my fighter, and I needed to help him out of this jam.

"Who are these guys who wanted Joey to throw the fight?" I asked.

"Local . . . businessmen who have invested in Bruiser's career, really shady characters who've been keeping an eye on Joey for a while. Once they heard he had a kid for a sponsor, they thought he'd be a soft touch to throw the fight and make some easy money."

"Like how you thought it would be easy to take the lawn business away from me?" I folded my arms and glared.

Rock ducked his head. "Yeah. It's just that, well, no one expects a kid to be doing the kinds of things you're doing."

Including me.

"Do you know anything about them?" I asked. "Anything that will help us figure out a way to get them to leave Joey alone?"

"I know that they're greedy."

"That could work in our favor," Arnold said. Behind that laid-back attitude and happy face, Arnold was nobody's fool.

"And Zed is part of that crew," Rock said.

"I knew he was up to no good," I said. "His story about being family is bogus."

Rock handed me a piece of paper. "I'd really like to help, so I made a list of names and addresses for you. Joey got me out of that bad crowd. Even washing urinals is better than hanging around with those people."

I studied the list and smiled. I handed the names to Arnold, who opened his computer and started tapping away.

"Are you thinking what I'm thinking?" I asked him.

"We need a team meeting."

"Exactly. All hands on deck."

13

Crisis Management as a Form of Team Building

An hour later we were all crowded around Arnold's picnic table—me, Arnold, Rock, Kenny, Allen, Savannah, Lindy, Gib, Frank and Kathy. And the lawn team, Pasqual, Louis and Benny. In the meantime, Arnold and I had figured out a plan.

We couldn't go up against these guys in terms of force because we weren't, you know, violent criminals. We weren't sure it would help to report them to the cops, because no one likes a rat. And they could come after us for that later. We just needed to make enough trouble for Bruiser and his crew that they'd lose interest in hassling Joey and Grandma.

66

"Okay, here's the deal," I said when everyone had squeezed around the table. "We need to . . . um . . . neutralize our opponents, and I'm looking to each of you to, uh, play to your strengths."

Arnold and I handed everyone a copy of the list of names and addresses that Rock had given us.

"Savannah: Arnold and I want you to make an anonymous call to the people at the tax office," I said, "and alert them to some underreporting of income by these individuals.

"Lindy, let those attorneys who were here this afternoon know about the, uh, civil liberties violations these guys have made because they, I don't know, abuse their employees by . . . withholding overtime pay. Or something. You'll think of the right thing.

"Kathy, call your friends at the newspapers and TV and radio stations and tip them off about the crooked betting ring in this town."

She sat up. "It's crying out to be exposed by the media!"

"Frank and Gib, Arnold says you used to work for a bunch of lawyers. Call as many as you can, tell them you're thinking about hiring them and that you want to sue the guys on the list for, oh, noise violations or unlicensed house pets. That way the attorneys can't be hired by any of the bad guys later. That's—" I looked at Arnold.

"—potential conflict of interest," he finished.

"Allen and Kenny, tell your folks you're spending the night with me. Tonight when it gets late, really late, like so late it's actually early morning, you go with Rock. Allen, bring your iPod and speakers, with the remote that you rigged to be super-powerful from a distance. Set the speakers high in the trees in Bruiser's yard—Pasqual and the guys will have hidden a ladder in the bushes—and don't forget to import that demo of Kenny's band from camp, Infected Wound. You can sit with Rock in his car—it has tinted windows so no one will be able to see you. Blast the demo. Then stop. Play it again a few more seconds. Wait a little longer. Crank the volume a couple more minutes—it's Chinese water torture by way of headbanging music."

"Awesome." Neither guy blinked at being instructed to join up with a reformed gangster who smelled strongly of urinal cakes to prank a former heavyweight champion prizefighter.

"Pasqual, Louis, Benny, these people need some yard work done. The kind that includes the improper disposal of all the animal waste you've collected from all the yards, you know, the accidental over-fertilization of the lawn directly under open windows. And if those windows have been mistakenly superglued open with the glue left over from Allen's science project last spring, well, it's an imperfect world, isn't it?

"Arnold is going to be researching their financial histories to assist Savannah and Lindy in creating legal nuisances for them.

"Okay, is everyone clear?" Nods all around the table.

"What about Zed?" Rock asked.

"Leave Zed," I said, "to me."

14

The Abrupt Termination of Proven Liabilities, with Some Pain

I was sitting in the kitchen the next morning eating cereal and looking off into the distance, counting the number of girls in the front yard wanting my autograph. Kenny and Allen had gotten back to my house about a half hour earlier, after a long night of band blasting.

"You should have heard it, man, it was great!" Kenny said. "We set the speakers up in the trees, dumped the ladders back where Pasqual had put them and then boogied to Rock's car. Bangbangbang, heavy metal blare. Dead silence. Wait for

70

it . . . wait for it . . . wait for it: Bangbangbangbang-bang heavy metal blare. Dead silence. The lights in the house were flipping on and off all night long and this big scary guy kept coming outside with a flashlight, looking for us."

"Rock ordered pizza and soda. I didn't know that Tony P's Pizza Palace would deliver to cars in the street." Allen looked happy.

"Then we peed in the empty soda bottles." Kenny looked even happier about that part of the story.

They grabbed some toast and headed out to the girls. I stared at my cereal.

Just then, Zed walked in, a towel wrapped around his middle and a toothbrush in his mouth. Looking good. The towel was so low in the back that I could see butt hairs in the crack. Groovy. I put my cereal down. Forever.

"Hey, dude, got coffee?"

"What are you doing?"

"Your granny said it was okay to shower in the house cuz my rig doesn't have one, which is okay cuz I don't take many showers."

Color me shocked.

"You spoke to her this morning?"

"She stopped by the rig on her way ta Joey's workout." Zed helped himself to a bowl of cereal, and the towel slipped lower as he reached for the milk. Please, I thought, please—no lower.

"I was looking forward to speaking with you," I said. "How are you and Joey related, again?"

"Oh"—he waved his hand—"you know. . . ."

Well, no, I don't know, which is why I asked. But before I could say anything, he went on.

"I'm a bettin' man and I bet my last dollar you gotta place fer a fella like me in yer organization."

And I'm betting you're *on* your last dollar.

"Look," he said, "just think about it. I'm havin' a few buddies over later ta, you know, hang out. Whyn'tcha come on out ta the rig, meet everyone, get some grub, and we can talk business?"

Before I could say no, not ever, unless you boil me in oil, he left the kitchen scratching his underarms and then—I winced—his butt.

That went well, I thought. Yeah, I seized control of the situation.

But I didn't have time to deal with Zed right then because I had to distribute paychecks to the work crews and I had a lot of ground to cover after I picked up the checks from Arnold's house. I had to tell each crew that there might be a slight disruption of business while we got some financial details ironed out.

This took more time than I thought it would. Mostly because everyone wanted to have their picture taken with me to show their families that they really did work for the kid in the news.

But that was just as well, because all day long I dreaded dealing with Zed, even though the rest of the team had done their bits during the day. I kept telling myself that all I had to do was point out that there was no place in Joey's career, my organization or our driveway for the likes of him. I knew that a well-structured argument would be my best weapon.

It was either that or hit him with a car axle.

As I drove up to my house on my lawn mower, I saw that our driveway and most of the front yard were packed with rusted-out pieces of automobiles. It looked like a junkyard—no, a tailgate party for a really bad demolition derby. Someone had pitched a tent in the side yard, and I was amazed to see a seating area with furniture from my house. My mother would have freaked if she'd seen all those grubby people sitting on her good sofa with their dirty boots on her coffee table, let alone that her living room set was now crowded in with the out-door furniture on the side patio.

And there were twenty, no, thirty, no, fifty or so people making themselves at home in our yard. I had never seen so many exposed beer bellies, home-made tattoos and butt cracks in my life. A bunch of people were sitting around a kiddie pool they'd filled with ice and cans of beer. One guy was taking a whiz against the side of the garage.

Loose dogs were milling around. I was horrified to see that one of them was eating a child—but it turned out to be a doll. The dogs were peeing too, and Pasqual would probably burst into tears when he saw what these mangy beasts had done to his beautiful grass.

Five portable grills were set up on the driveway. People were standing over them cooking hot dogs on sticks and what looked like skinned possum or some other source of protein not usually found in butcher shops. And everyone was eating that slop off my mother's good dishes from her china cabinet in the dining room.

I heard Grandma's voice and wheeled around. She was talking to Zed. He had his arm draped around her shoulders, and my blood ran cold. She was supposed to be with Joey, not here, not with Zed, not with Zed touching her.

Zed slipped his hand into her purse.

I jammed the lawn mower into rabbit gear and went storming up the driveway, screeching to a stop in front of Zed.

"I know that you work for Bruiser and his people."

The entire party fell silent.

"I don't work fer Bruiser; I jus' know him 'n' his friends."

"The same friends who expected Joey Pow to throw the fight."

"You talk like that's a bad thing."

"And take your hands off my grandmother. Joey might not be here to protect her, but no one's going to hurt Grandma."

"You think you can stop me?"

That was when Grandma slugged him.

Slugged him so hard that he dropped to his knees and then fell to his side and curled up in a fetal position, making high-pitched whistling sounds.

While Zed rocked back and forth clutching his side and gasping for breath, I circled his guests on the lawn mower, herding them up like a border collie herds sheep—if border collies drove riding mowers and the sheep were scary redneck white trash—and forcing them to the dented rust buckets they called their cars. After a few loud minutes of people cursing, car motors grinding and backfiring, everyone had gone.

Zed, without a word or so much as a glance in our direction, crawled to his truck, backed out of the driveway and headed down the street.

"Grandma, you punched Zed in the gut!"

"No, dear, it was the kidney. It's extreme, and not proper in the ring, but a very effective tool when you're under attack. He'll pee blood for several days, but he'll never show up to make trouble for Joey again."

"How do you know about punching kidneys?"

"Joey taught me. The secret is to keep your wrist straight and aim two feet past the target and get the weight of your shoulder into the blow. And when you make chocolate Bundt cake with the river of pudding in the middle, it's important to remember to use the cook-and-serve pudding and not the instant mix or it's not so much a river as it is thin ooze, and no one wants that on their dessert plate."

Grandma is never lacking in life lessons and surprises.

15

The Perils of Free Enterprise

Luckily, Allen and Kenny stopped by and helped clean up. We had just finished picking up all the garbage and dog poop from the yard and dragging the furniture back into the house. It almost looked like we'd never played host to the Souls of the Damned convention. Allen and Kenny rode off on their bikes just as my parents drove up the driveway.

The car had barely stopped before they tumbled out and threw their arms around me and Grandma, hugging and kissing and telling us how long the five days away from us had seemed.

Five days.

It felt like I'd lived several centuries since they'd left.

Zed had arrived and departed.

My staff had expanded.

Lawyers had filed papers.

Tax problems had erupted.

My staff had become a bunch of organized trouble-makers to scare off some bad guys.

Grandma had thrown a kidney punch.

My parents looked calm and happy.

The exact opposite of how I felt.

"We have so much to tell you, it's been so thrilling—life-changing, really," my mother said.

That was how I'd describe my last week too.

"We found a little cottage on the north shore of a lake," Dad explained. "You can see the sunrise over the east shore and the sunset along the western horizon."

Grandma said, "It's no use boiling your cabbage twice."

After we shot each other a confused look, Mom picked up the story.

"It's got a screened-in porch where we can eat breakfast and watch the lake," she said. "And a stone fireplace and three little bedrooms with built-in bookcases. The nights are so quiet and dark that you can hear the leaves rustle on the trees and there are more stars in the sky than you ever imagined."

"And you can spend a lot of time in the fresh air." They both said this at the same time. My parents are big on me spending time in the fresh air.

"But that's not the life-changing part—" Dad started before I cut him off.

"Listen, Mom, Dad, I waited too long earlier this summer to tell you what was going on with my business. So I need to interrupt and bring you up to date on Zed and the lawsuits."

"Who's Zed?" Dad asked.

"Lawsuits?" Mom looked worried.

"And the staff and the tax audit and the media attention and the people who wanted Joey to throw the fight, too."

Dad put his hand on my shoulder. "Let's go inside, sit down and talk."

They sat quietly and listened. As for me, hearing myself say it all out loud, one horrible fact after another, was almost too much. Even having resolved the Zed thing, and working as I was to fix the Bruiser situation, I felt like there were just too many problems. It would take a million years to make everything quiet and smooth like before. And I was never going to get to ride my bike again, no matter how many new inner tubes I could afford.

Dad said, "We'll just have to take it one day at a time."

Mom took my hand and patted it. "Nothing is ever as bad as it seems, dear."

"We'll talk to Arnold and the tax people and the lawyers and figure this out." Dad looked confident.

"I'm sure it's just a matter of explaining to the right people," Mom said.

How could they be so serene and matter-of-fact about these disasters? Had I told the story right? My parents should have freaked out. That was what I was doing.

I wanted to run away.

No. Wait.

It was time to do some thinking.

16

Accumulation of Wealth Through Inheritance

So I went to the garage to sit on my lawn mower.

Only I was too riled up to sit. I kicked the tires and I pounded the seat. In fact, I hit the seat so hard that I loosened something, which fluttered to the ground.

A small plastic bag had been duct-taped to the underside of the seat. I stared at it for a few seconds before ripping open the plastic. A folded paper fell out.

A ship is safe in the harbor, but that's not why ships are built.

This was written in clean block letters, perfectly

formed, the way a kindergarten teacher would print. Or the way a man who always took good care of his tools would print. Clear and sharp.

My grandfather.

What did ships have to do with lawn mowers, and why would he go to the trouble to write this sentence down and then carefully hide it underneath the seat? I had suddenly found a clue to a scavenger hunt I didn't know I had joined.

I climbed back on the lawn mower to study the . . . proverb, I guess you'd call it. It sounded familiar.

It sounded like Grandma.

I did what I do when she says stuff I don't understand—I sat back and waited for the meaning to become clear.

I waited.

And I waited some more.

I waited just a tad longer.

Finally, I realized that my heart wasn't pounding and my breathing had slowed down. I didn't feel like yelling or kicking or pounding anymore.

I still felt like running away, though.

Away.

Had Grandpa been trying to tell me to run away to sea? I hoped not, because I get seasick really easily and, from what I hear, boats seem to require endless repairs and maintenance, and I was already at the edge of my performance envelope making sure the lawn mower had enough gas and oil. I'm just not machine oriented.

Sailing didn't sound particularly calming and soothing to me, at least not now. Maybe when I was older.

There must be another purpose to this note from Grandpa.

The words sounded simple and wise and wonderful. And I was all for those qualities coming to stay with me for a while.

I never really knew my grandfather, but the lawn mower had come from him. He'd gotten me into this situation, and I hoped this was his way of getting me out.

Maybe the meaning of the message wasn't in what he said, but in how he said it, and he was telling me to keep things simple.

If I was being honest, I'd have to admit he hadn't gotten me into this situation—I'd gotten myself into it. And I needed to get myself out. And do what I felt was right for me and my family.

I took a deep breath and got off my lawn mower.

I wiped it down, making sure to remove clods of dried mud and clumps of grass from the under-carriage and chipping the dried dirt off the pictures of the rabbit and the turtle. The lawn mower had seen better days, but in the dim light of the over-head bulb in the garage, it seemed to glow.

Then I went back into the house to speak to Mom and Dad and Grandma about what we needed to do to shift our lives back to turtle mode.

17

Leadership for Social Change and Renewal

I called a staff meeting for first thing the next morning. Arnold, Pasqual, Louis, Benny, Joey, Gib, Savannah, Frank, Lindy, Kathy, Kenny, Allen, Rock, Mom, Dad and Grandma crammed into Arnold's screened-in porch.

I stood up at the table and cleared my throat.

"I'm just a simple working man. I'm not even a man. I'm just a kid who wanted to make enough money this summer to buy a new inner tube for his bike."

They all stared up at me. Gib was taking notes for a report he'd later write and share with the team.

I hoped he didn't miss a word.

"I can't do this anymore—too many employees, tax problems, lawsuits, greedy fake relatives, interviews and autograph seekers. I'm sick of it."

I took a deep breath and faced Arnold. "I'm out."

I heard a gasp from Kathy. And then she started thumb-typing on her BlackBerry, no doubt canceling the appearances she'd set up. Everyone else was silent.

"Give Pasqual and Louis and Benny the lawn service. Do what you need to do so that Joey finds another sponsor or make sure he has enough money so he doesn't need a new one. I don't want franchises and endorsements and publicity anymore, so we need to find Kathy and Gib and Frank other jobs. Let Savannah and Lindy and Arnold focus on their other clients. Shut down the whole thing. Cash out and put the money in some fund that I can't touch until college.

"I'm done. I quit."

No one said anything. No one blinked. Even Kathy had stopped texting.

"My mom and dad and I talked last night. We're going up north to a little place they found on the lake until school starts in a couple of weeks. I'm going to ride my bike, have some kind of summer vacation that's not about work and money and craziness."

My parents and Grandma were the only ones smiling at me.

"I can't thank you all enough for all the good work you've done, especially you, Arnold. This whole thing was because of you—not the bad parts, of course, but all the money and the expansion and the staff. You did an amazing job. All of you did. But I'm twelve years old and I just want to have a summer vacation."

Grandma said, "It's no use carrying an umbrella if your shoes are leaking. And, hon"—she winked— "no one can ever blame a man for following his own heart and making the decision he knows is right. A ship is safe in the harbor. . . ."

18

The Theorem of
What Comes Next

We were packed and out of the house later that morning. We discovered that Zed had come back while we were out and taken the china he'd used for his party and most of Mom's good towels, which he'd used after his showers (we honestly didn't want those back). He'd also taken the easy chair, the big television from the den and every single battery, flashlight and lightbulb in the house, as well as the contents of the deep freeze in the garage.

The only hassle was getting my lawn mower hitched to the back of our car. I couldn't see leaving it behind.

We settled into the cabin in no time flat. Mom spent a lot of time reading, and Dad got the shed set up so he could work on inventions, and I made a couple of new friends. We hung out at the frozen custard stand and they came over to fish with me.

The cabin came with a small sailboat tied to the end of the dock, so I was teaching myself to sail. After about the twelfth time I tipped over or got stuck in the middle of the lake waiting for the wind to come up and blow me back to shore, I wondered: Would I have attempted to learn about the sailboat if I hadn't found the note from Grandpa?

I didn't hear from anyone who'd been at that last staff meeting except Grandma. How come? Were they all so busy dismantling operations that they didn't have time to get in touch, or were they all mad at me and did they never want to talk to me again?

Life had become quiet and peaceful, and I felt like hundreds of pounds of pressure had been lifted from my shoulders. I told myself I wasn't the kind of guy who was meant to be rich. That I didn't need the money and I could live without it just fine.

I missed the work, though. I felt weird, kind of

guilty, sleeping in every morning, and all day long I kept checking my watch, as if I had a yard to get to. And I wondered what everyone was doing. I had a tough time falling asleep every night too. Now that I wasn't exhausted all the time, sleep didn't come as easy and deep as it had.

I started to count the days until we could get back home and I could start school. I didn't even mind the prospect of facing trig.

Grandma showed up for dinner the second week. She brought me an old-fashioned hand-cranked ice cream machine and said, "There's no need to fear the wind if your haystacks are tied down."

I was getting better at translating Grandma-speak and asked, "Was this Grandpa's too?"

"Yes. Your grandpa loved ice cream. He always said no one ever matched his vanilla kumquat recipe, which just goes to show that wooden shoe trees don't help a bit when it's time to vote."

"Ah, yes, well . . ." I was studying the crank and wondering where to find instructions for making ice cream by hand. I'd noticed that the lakeside town up the road didn't have a decent ice cream parlor.

I started to get that buzzy itch in the back of my head like when I first started the lawn business. Kenny and Allen could come up with us next summer, and if we could start a little stand near the town square . . .

19

The Axiom of
Shifting Paradigms

I was fishing off the edge of the dock outside our cabin the day we were going to head back home. The sun had just come up and the lake was smooth and still.

"Far-out place you've got here."

Arnold.

I turned and saw him standing at the top of the dock. Short and round and dressed in one of those awful outfits from way back when—bell-bottom pants and a sports coat with enormous lapels.

And easily one of the best things I've ever seen in my whole entire life.

He smiled and kind of waved when our eyes met and then he walked down to sit next to me, our legs hanging over the side of the dock.

"I thought you'd be angry with me. Or disappointed," I told him.

"Not at all. I blame myself, if you want to know the truth. I kept forgetting you were only twelve and I put responsibilities and obligations on you and made you vulnerable to all sorts of issues and problems that would break a grown man. I just got so caught up in the beauty of the system and how groovy it was all working out."

"What"—the words caught in my throat— "what happened to everyone? I've been worried about how I left things and if they could all find new jobs."

"That's what I came to tell you." Arnold smiled. "I kept them all on for my business."

"What do you mean?"

"You're not the only one who benefited from the media exposure and financial success, you know."

"Oh, sure."

"I made the same investments with my money that I did with yours so that we had the same risk and, as it turned out, the identical rewards, too. I've

93

been drawing a commission from your stock and bond transactions in addition to the other consulting and investment work I've always done. Pasqual and the rest of the crew and Joey Pow and the office staff all invest with me. I've been conservative, in this market, but even so they're not hurting for additional sources of income on top of salary and wages."

"I'm glad to hear that things are working out."

"I'm going to buy that building downtown. I'll take up the top floor and I'll rent two offices to Savannah and Lindy. And I'll rent out the other two floors to an architecture firm and a graphic design company. A nice income from rent."

"That's wonderful. How're Pasqual, Louis, Benny and the rest of the guys? I've been worrying about them now that fall is coming. No more lawn mowing."

"PLB, Inc. PLB, of course, stands for Pasqual and Lawn Boy." He smiled again when he saw my face light up. "The company is doing really well. Not only did the publicity increase the demand for their lawn services, but they're going to expand into snowplowing in the winter months. They've purchased their first two plows and have three more on order."

"Ahh. It's all taken care of. . . ."

"Wait. There's more: They insisted that you continue to collect your percentage on the business earnings. So you have remained a silent partner in the expanded operations. They believe it wouldn't be right to go on without you. Every member of the team voted to keep you on and honor your efforts by adding your name to the company."

"Wow. I had no idea. I don't know what to say."

"They're good men. Hard workers. Loyal. They know about respect and honor and standing to with their friends."

"How's Joey?"

"Your grandmother hasn't told you her news?"

I shook my head. Grandma had news? And had kept it to herself? Well, maybe she'd thought she told me when she started talking about how you trim a cat's toenails.

"In the heat of the moment, I forgot to tell you that she had given me forty dollars to invest awhile back, and, well, luck with investments sure does run in your family. We've turned that modest amount into quite a little nest egg. Nothing along the lines of what you've made, of course—that would be impossible. But enough so that she can have some fun."

"What kind of fun?"

"Joey Pow kind of fun. She's his new sponsor. And she hired Rock to take over as his manager. They arrange his bouts, set up his travel plans and work with his trainers to make sure he's in top physical shape. She's training too, in a modest way, and she's gotten a new lease on life. Joey is very happy. Those two have a unique connection. They're good for each other."

"Yeah, I guess they are."

"Oh, and speaking of Joey: He found out that you found out that Zed had threatened your grandmother. He was very upset that his sponsor had been worried and, suffice it to say, Zed's threat has been terminated."

"Just the threat, right? Joey didn't, you know, actually . . . terminate . . . Zed?"

"There was some head pinching, and Zed won't be able to eat solid foods for three to six weeks, but there isn't any lasting physical damage. The psychological afteraffects might be permanent. Which would be good. In the meantime, Joey hired Zed so he could supervise him like he did Rock, because he says it's important to keep your friends close and your not-friends even closer."

"Joey is brilliant. He's good people, too."

"How are you?" Arnold asked me. "Everything groovy up here for you and your folks?"

"This is the greatest place. I'm really glad my folks bought it."

"That's something I should explain. Because they have powers of attorney, your parents can withdraw from your accounts to provide adequate housing for you while you are a minor. So this cabin is yours, free and clear. They bought it for you."

"I own the cabin?"

"And the entire lake."

"I own a lake?"

"Yes, and a few acres surrounding the shoreline."

"What about those little cabins on the other shore?"

"They're part of the resort. Your resort."

"I own a resort?"

"Yes, you do. A very small one. Turns out if we'd simply cashed out of the market and put the money in savings, we would have taken a tax hit that I found unacceptable. Your parents agreed that rein-vesting in property was the right thing. You didn't lose money, but this kind of investment won't add the same kind of pressure that the stock market put on you."

"So . . . wait . . . I'm still making money from the lawn care business and now there's going to be more money from the snowplow business *and* I own a resort?"

He nodded and smiled.

"And everybody's job is safe?"

"Yes."

"What about the audit and the frozen assets?"

"I told you that Lindy and Savannah were the best in the business. They made those problems dis-appear. We'd always kept impeccable books, and once the situation was laid out in full for the tax of-fice, we were A-OK."

"How about the guys who told Joey to throw the fight?"

"Remember the lawyers who wanted you to sue everyone?" I flinched and nodded. "Well, they're filing injunctions right and left, tying all those guys up in red tape. Those guys are too busy to scheme. Plus, they're in a world of trouble with the tax people. It's going to take them a lot of time and money, maybe some jail time, to resolve all these issues. The legal system can be, at times, groovy."

"That's cool."

He pulled a small notebook out of his jacket pocket.

"You've always given me a free hand with your investments and trusted me to have your best interests at heart."

"Of course."

"I hope you'll agree with the decisions I made on your behalf. I kept reinvesting the money; I'm a stockbroker and it goes against everything I stand for to drop out of the game when it's going so well. Frankly, I can't understand it, but no matter what happens elsewhere in this crazy market, your investments continue to do well."

"Am I still rich?"

"Yup. And your parents and I set up a trust fund. You can't touch it for any reason, not even to give it away, until you're twenty-five. The money is safe and making interest for you. Plus, there's the college fund. And your retirement plans. All immutable—that means you can't change them. And untouchable."

"So how much am I worth?"

He licked his finger and paged through the small notebook he held.

"Well, remember we started out with a forty-dollar investment? And that morphed into eight thousand dollars?"

"And change, yes. But that was gross and not net."

He smiled because I'd been paying attention and remembered what he'd taught me. "And then the eight became sixteen and we reinvested it in a high-risk stock that went crazy?"

"And that's when the investments grew to about fifty thousand dollars plus the eight I'd made from the lawns."

"And change," we both said.

"Then, of course, that sell order didn't go through and there was a merger and so you were, at that point, worth something in the neighborhood of four hundred and eighty thousand dollars."

"And change," we said together.

"Right."

"Well, since I continued investing half of that amount, a conservative estimate, including partial ownership of the expanded lawn service, your investments, the property and your grandmother's earnings from stocks and Joey, which she funneled

100

back into your trust rather than keeping it herself, you've cracked the million-dollar ceiling."

"And change."

"Sure. There's always change."

And change, I thought, looking out across a lake I owned, is always good.

ABOUT THE AUTHOR

Gary Paulsen is the distinguished author of many critically acclaimed books for young people, including three Newbery Honor Books: *The Winter Room*, *Hatchet*, and *Dogsong*. He won the Margaret A. Edwards Award given by the ALA for his lifetime achievement in young adult literature. Among his Random House Books are *Liar, Liar*; *Masters of Disaster*; *Woods Runner*; *Lawn Boy*; *Lawn Boy Returns*; *Notes from the Dog*; *Mudshark*; *The Legend of Bass Reeves*; *The Amazing Life of Birds*; *The Time Hackers*; *Molly McGinty Has a Really Good Day*; *The Quilt* (a companion to *Alida's Song* and *The Cookcamp*); *How Angel Peterson Got His Name*; *Guts: The True Stories Behind* Hatchet *and The Brian Books*; *The Beet Fields*; *Soldier's Heart*; *Brian's Return*, *Brian's Winter*, and *Brian's Hunt* (companions to *Hatchet*); *Father Water, Mother Woods*; and five books about Francis Tucket's adventures in the Old West. Gary Paulsen has also published fiction and nonfiction for adults. His wife, Ruth Wright Paulsen, is an artist who has illustrated several of his books. He divides his time between his home in Alaska, his ranch in New Mexico, and his sailboat on the Pacific Ocean. You can visit him on the Web at GaryPaulsen.com.

YEARLING HUMOR!

Looking for more funny books to read?
Check these out!

- ❏ *Bad Girls* by Jacqueline Wilson
- ❏ Calvin Coconut: *Trouble Magnet* by Graham Salisbury
- ❏ *Don't Make Me Smile* by Barbara Park
- ❏ *Fern Verdant and the Silver Rose* by Diana Leszczynski
- ❏ *Funny Frank* by Dick King-Smith
- ❏ *Gooney Bird Greene* by Lois Lowry
- ❏ *How Tía Lola Came to ~~Visit~~ Stay* by Julia Alvarez
- ❏ *How to Save Your Tail* by Mary Hanson
- ❏ *I Was a Third Grade Science Project* by Mary Jane Auch

- ❏ *Jelly Belly* by Robert Kimmel Smith
- ❏ *Lawn Boy* by Gary Paulsen
- ❏ *Nim's Island* by Wendy Orr
- ❏ *Out of Patience* by Brian Meehl
- ❏ Shredderman: *Secret Identity* by Wendelin Van Draanen
- ❏ *Toad Rage* by Morris Gleitzman
- ❏ *A Traitor Among the Boys* by Phyllis Reynolds Naylor